This book belongs to

....

igloo

This edition published in 2011
by Igloo Books Ltd
Cottage Farm
Sywell
NN6 0BJ
www.igloo-books.com

www.humphreys-corner.com

B044 0211

2 4 6 8 10 9 7 5 3 1
ISBN: 978-0-85734-598-1

Printed and manufactured in China

Humphrey's Farm Adventure

Sally Hunter

It was a lovely, sunny day and Mummy had taken Humphrey and his little friend, Tilly, to the farm on Duffy's Hill.

Humphrey wanted to go and see the animals straight away, but Mum said, "Let's have our picnic first."

Humphrey was too excited
to finish all his lunch.
He kept his apple for later.

Mum bought some animal
feed and filled up Humphrey's
and Tilly's buckets. "Let's go!"
shouted Humphrey.

First of all, Humphrey and Tilly
said hello to the sheep.

They were very pleased to see
them, especially with the treats!

Humphrey liked the baby
lamb the best.

Sheep

The ducks made a lot of quacking noises when they saw Humphrey.

Humphrey said they must like
him very much, because they
followed him down the path.

Duck

Humphrey and Tilly thought
the pigs were very cute!

There were five little
piglets, too. They had floppy,
pink ears and curly tails.

Tilly wanted really badly
to take one home.

Pig

The cows were nice and friendly
and seemed very interested
in Humphrey and Tilly.

"I think they like our snacks
more than the grass!" said Tilly.

Humphrey made friends with the
smallest one. He called him Moo.

Cow

Next, Humphrey said hello to
the chickens. They made
clucking noises and wanted to
see what was in his bucket!

Oh! There is a VERY cheeky one!
She found Humphrey's treats and
decided to finish them up!

Oh, dear! That's all the
snacks gone and Humphrey
and Tilly still needed to
visit Henry the Horse.

Chicken

What a good job Humphrey
still had his apple. Henry had
the nicest treat of all!

Tilly stroked Henry
on his soft nose.

Horse

Humphrey and Tilly have said
hello to all the animals.

Mum made them wash
their hands two times.

Then they were allowed to choose
a farm book each, from the gift shop.
Humphrey and Tilly have had
a wonderful day at the farm.

Can you remember all the animals Humphrey and Tilly have seen today?

Sheep

Cow

Chicken

Duck

Pig

Horse

Goodbye,
farm animals!

Goodbye, Tilly.

Goodbye, Humphrey.
See you soon!